Speckle
The Stray

Jenny Oldfield

Illustrated by Kate Aldous

Hodder
Children's
Books

a division of Hodder Headline plc

A Catalogue record for this book is available from the British Libra

ISBN 0 340 66127 5

Typeset by Avon Dataset Ltd, Bidford-on-Avon, Warks

Printed and bound in Great Britain by
The Guernsey Press Co. Ltd, Guernsey, Channel Islands

Hodder Children's Books
a division of Hodder Headline plc
338 Euston Road
London NW1 3BH

SPECKLE
The Stray

One

'Are we here yet?' Helen Moore asked her dad for the umpteenth time.

'No, sit still.' David Moore drove steadily through Doveton village.

'How long before we're there, then?' Helen's twin sister, Hannah, peered over his shoulder. The road ahead was narrow and steep.

'Not long,' their mum promised.

'You said that two hours ago!' Helen didn't like being stuck in the car. She loved exploring and finding things out for herself.

Hannah spotted a farmhouse up ahead. 'Is this it?'

1

A dog barked at the gate, a ginger tom-cat sat on a stone wall.

Helen tutted. 'How can it be? Home Farm is empty.'

Hannah pulled a face. 'So?'

'So how could there be a cat and dog there, stupid?'

'No fighting!' Mary Moore warned. She folded the map she'd used to find their way. 'We're nearly there. Home Farm is just at the top of this hill.'

'Fell,' David Moore corrected her. 'This is the Lake District. They call their hills fells round here.'

Hannah and Helen could hardly wait. Soon the car came to a stop by a broken farm gate. Hannah saw the apple blossom petals drift across the empty farmyard. Helen saw the wild heather on the hills beyond.

'Is this it?' Helen cried, flinging Henry, her favourite stuffed dog, to the floor in her hurry.

Her dad drove into the farmyard. The gate was off its hinges, grass grew high between the flagstones.

'Home Farm!' Hannah picked Henry up and showed him the old sign nailed to the big chestnut tree by the gate.

'Home sweet home!' Helen grinned. Ivy crept up the white-washed walls and over the slate roof. A window was broken in the front of the old stone house.

Mary Moore opened the car door, got out and tilted her seat forward to set the twins free. 'Bring your sleeping-bags,' she told them. 'And leave the rest of that rubbish there until the morning.'

They climbed out, wrapping the warm bags round their shoulders. Helen was first, as usual. She turned to wait for Hannah, who carried Henry clasped under one arm.

One twin was a mirror image of the other. Their thick brown hair blown back by the wind, their big dark eyes sparkling with the thrill of being there, even though they'd been driving for hours in the cramped, clattery car. They'd come all the way from their city home to this new one in the country, if you could call such an old house new. It was falling apart and had one boarded-up window.

Dusk had almost fallen, and there wasn't much time to explore. The clear sky was tinged with pink. Down below, at the start of the road they'd just climbed, a lake glittered silver in the evening light.

Their dad stood beside their mum. He stretched after the long drive. 'Peace and quiet!' he sighed.

This was why he'd come to live in the country. He could carry on working as a photographer from here, and send his pictures by post to the newspaper and magazine offices in London.

'Away from the rat race,' she agreed. Mary Moore was small, slight and dark, like the twins. She was the one who'd got them going on the idea of moving out to the Lake District. She'd grown up in the country, and told them all about the good life; the fields and hills, the woods and streams. 'It's my dream come true!'

'Off the beaten track.' Their dad folded his arms and gazed at the old farmhouse. 'Better fix that window first thing tomorrow,' he reminded himself.

Hannah took it all in; the ancient house, the wide open spaces. She turned to Helen. 'What do you think?'

Helen could hardly believe it. The house was on a mountain. They might call it a fell, but it was an actual mountain. 'It's ... big!' she gasped. 'All this ... countryside everywhere!' She was stuck for words to describe it.

'What do you want to see first?' Hannah rushed here and there. She peeked through windows and tried to open doors. There was so much to look at.

'Let's climb that fell thingy!' Helen fancied a quick dash up the mountain before dark. She ran to ask her mum. 'Can we explore?' she asked. The light was fading fast.

Mrs Moore frowned. 'Tomorrow.'

'Oh, Mum!'

'Tomorrow!' she said again, more firmly than before.

Hannah agreed. 'Come on, let's explore inside the house!' She dragged her sister towards the door, then stopped. 'Dad, will you take Henry?' She handed over the dog-eared bloodhound.

'Down, boy!' he commanded, with a growl and a scuff round the poor thing's head. He tucked it under his arm. 'Woof! Quiet! Down, boy!'

Helen grinned, then followed hot on Hannah's heels. They stepped over the threshold into Home Farm for the very first time.

Floorboards sounded hollow under their feet, hinges on doors creaked and groaned. Cobwebs hung from the kitchen ceiling and across the bare window. Hannah and Helen trod warily from room to room.

'Cree-py!' Helen whispered.

'Whoo-oo!' Hannah's voice echoed down the hall.

'I'm a ghost and I'm coming to get you!' Helen raised her arms and flapped them at Hannah as they climbed the creaky stairs.

'I'm not scared of you-oo!' Hannah flapped back.

'Boo!' David Moore popped his head round a bedroom door.

'Aagh!' The twins jumped a mile.

'Dad, don't do that!' Hannah cried.

'Where's the light switch?' Helen fumbled along the wall, glad when she found the landing light.

'Who wants a cup of hot chocolate?' their mum called from the kitchen.

'Me, please!' the twins chorused.

'And then it's bed for you two, and an early start tomorrow. The furniture van gets here at eight.'

Helen groaned and frowned round their empty bedroom. 'What bed does she mean?' The boards were bare, there was one little fireplace full of soot, and a sloping ceiling. Nothing else.

Hannah grinned. 'It looks like we're camping on the floor tonight!' This was great, she decided. No beds, no furniture. 'Bags this corner!' She squatted down on her chosen spot.

'Bags this one!' Helen took the corner opposite. Then she went and pressed her face against the dark window pane. Outside it was pitch black. Down the fell, a tiny yellow light glittered. 'Sca-ry!' she whispered.

They listened. There was wind in the trees and silence. No traffic. No people. Hannah shivered.

'Helen! Hannah!' Mary Moore called from downstairs.

'Coming!' they answered. All of a sudden, the bare house seemed a friendly place after all. It might have slates missing from the roof, and the barn door across the farmyard might bang in the wind. But they were safe from the dark inside Home Farm.

That evening, the lights at Home Farm glowed yellow through the bare windows.

The twins were glad when their father finally managed to light a fire in the kitchen grate. His face was grimy, his fawn jumper streaked with soot. The little yellow flames flickered, caught hold of the big logs, then roared loud and orange. David Moore stood back, wiping his hands on his trousers. 'That's more like it,' he said. 'I'd better fix that central heating boiler tomorrow. Will you remind me?' At the moment there was no way of heating the water in the tank.

Hannah curled up by the fire. She nodded sleepily. Her fingers were cupped around a warm mug of hot chocolate.

'Mum, the cold water's a mucky brown!' Helen called from the bathroom in disgust. 'I can't brush my teeth!'

'Leave it for tonight.' Mary Moore stood dreamily at the kitchen window, gazing out at the stars.

'I'll fix it tomorrow,' their dad promised.

Hannah smiled at Helen as she came down in her pyjamas. They'd both escaped the dreaded toothbrush.

'Window, gate, roof, boiler, water-pipes.' David Moore made a confident list of things to see to.

The twins knew their dad wasn't the sort who went round with a hammer and a screwdriver, mending things.

Helen grinned at Hannah. 'Dad, do you want us to help with the jobs?' She liked the idea of climbing on to the roof with him.

He yawned. 'Oh, I don't know about that. You see,

most of these things need to be tackled by an expert.'

Hannah glanced at her mum and swallowed a laugh. 'An expert?'

'Yes, someone who knows what they're doing. It's skilled work, plumbing and working with wood and suchlike. Unless, of course, you have a kind of natural talent for working with your hands.'

'Like you did when you made our bookshelves in the old house?' Hannah reminded him. The twins loved to tease their dad.

Helen screeched with laughter. 'Yes, and when it was finished, and we put three books and Henry on it, it fell to bits!' They rolled about. The idea of him mending the roof at Home Farm was hilarious.

David Moore laughed too. 'That was just a little slip-up,' he admitted. 'Anyway, Henry's such a great fat lump!' He thrust the toy dog at Hannah. 'Woof!'

The twins jumped on their dad and wrestled him.

'Time for bed, you two,' their mum told them at last.

Still giggling, the twins climbed the narrow stairs to their new bedroom. Soon they were curled inside their sleeping-bags on the bare floorboards.

Their mum came up to turn off the light. 'Sleep

well.' She propped Henry on the windowsill.

'Mum . . .' Hannah opened one eye.

'What?'

'This is great. Home Farm and everything . . .'

' . . . But?' Mary Moore waited, one hand on the light switch.

'Well, there's something missing.'

'Beds!' Helen muttered, trying to get comfy on the hard floor.

'No!'

'Carpets, curtains, lightshades, chairs, drawers, wardrobes!' Home Farm wasn't exactly a home yet.

'No! Shut up, Helen!' Hannah propped herself on her elbows.

'What then?' Their mum sounded tired.

'Animals. You know; cows and sheep and things.' Home Farm wasn't exactly a farm without them.

Since she was tiny, Hannah had loved animals. In town, in their cramped terraced house near to the main road, she'd had to grit her teeth and accept the family's 'no pets' rule. She'd made do with a whole zoo of stuffed toys instead. But now they were in the country she hoped the rule would change.

'I mean, maybe we can't have cows, but shouldn't

Home Farm have a cat and a dog at least?'

Mary Moore smiled. She came and knelt by Hannah's sleeping-bag. 'Nice try, Hann. But you'll have to be patient. I've got to work at The Curlew every day, remember.' She'd taken on a little health food cafe in Nesfield, the local town. She would be too busy at first to look after any pets. 'And your dad will have his hands full here, getting the house in order.'

Hannah sighed.

'Sorry. Animals will just have to wait.' Their mum gave them both a kiss. She went out quietly and closed the door.

In the dark, Helen made a popping sound with her lips. 'Call this a farm!' she whispered in disgust. What was the point of moving out here if they couldn't keep animals?

'Helen?' Hannah's voice was quavery.

'What?'

'If I show you something, will you keep it secret?'

The moon shone through the small window. It cast a pale, cold light. 'What is it?'

Hannah raised an arm out of her sleeping-bag and held an object up to the light. It was loop-shaped. 'This. I found it hanging on a hook on the kitchen door.'

Helen stared hard. 'It's a dog's collar. What's it doing here?'

'The old owners must have left it.' Hannah handed the precious collar to her sister.

'But I thought the house had been empty for ages.' Helen squinted at a smooth metal disk hanging from the worn leather collar. 'What's it say on this name tag? I can't read it.'

Hannah unzipped her sleeping-bag and crept close. 'The writing's worn down. It's pretty old.'

'Like everything else round here.' The tag gleamed in the moonlight. 'Look, it starts with an "S".'

' "Speckle", that's what it says. It must be the dog's name.'

'Speckle,' Helen repeated. She pictured a black and white sheepdog with a long, flowing tail, ears flat to its head, loping across the lakeside fells.

'If I had a dog, that's what I'd call it,' Hannah said.

'Even if it was all black?'

She ignored this. 'The collar was what made me ask Mum about having a pet.'

'Well, she said no!' Helen sounded cross.

Sulking, Hannah retreated with the collar to her sleeping-bag.

'Sorry.' Helen hadn't meant to snap.

'It's OK.'

'Hannah?'

'What?'

'I want a dog just as much as you do, you know.'

There was a silence for a while.

'Maybe Mum will change her mind?' Helen held out a small hope.

'Or Dad.' This was a slightly larger hope. Their dad always had a smile in his grey eyes. When their mum said no, she meant it.

'A farm *needs* a dog!' Helen insisted. The edges of

her words were blurring with sleep.

'Definitely. I bet every other farm round here has one!'

'And a cat.'

'And chickens. Mum could have free range eggs for the shop!' Hannah was still wide awake.

'Mmm.' Helen drifted off.

Hannah lay for a long time with her eyes open. She heard the wind in the chestnut tree. An owl hooted. She *thought* it was an owl. The call didn't sound much like 'tu-whit-tu-whoo!', but what else could it be?

At last she too fell asleep. She dreamed of Speckle, the faithful old farm dog, fast asleep by a blazing fire. His son, Speckle Junior, played outside in the yard.

The twins woke next morning to the sound of a giant, square removal van chugging to a halt in the yard below. Two men jumped out and lowered the ramp. All morning they heaved and carried, drank tea, wiped their brows and began again. David Moore helped. Mary showed them exactly where things should go.

Meanwhile, Hannah and Helen escaped to the hills.

Two

'Let's go down to the lake!' Helen led the way. She saw sailing-boats and windsurfers, and a steamer chugging across the smooth surface.

They ran together down the hill, through a wood, into a small, open field. The boats still looked like white dots on the water. 'How far is it?' Hannah gasped. It hadn't seemed this far in the car. She could just see Doveton, with its church and single row of grey houses snaking along the water's edge.

'Not far.' Helen refused to be put off. She began to sprint across the field.

The twins were knee-deep in grass and buttercups

when they realised that the field belonged to someone. A goat stood in their path, feet planted wide apart, head down, horns pointed straight at them. They stopped dead in their tracks.

Helen and Hannah stared into the goat's amber eyes. They held their breath.

The brown goat pawed the ground with her hoof.

'What now?' Helen squeezed the words from between clenched teeth. 'Run?' She didn't fancy being charged by those spiky horns.

'Uh-uh.' Hannah shook her head. The gate out of the field was miles away. Anyhow, the goat had decided not to charge. She advanced slowly towards them.

They stood statue-still until they could feel the goat's hot breath, see the narrow slit-pupils of her yellow eyes, hear the quiet munch of her teeth as her jaws went on slowly chewing grass.

Helen inched closer towards Hannah. 'Why don't you stroke her?' she whispered.

'Me?'

'Yes, go on. She looks friendly.'

'Says you!' Still, Hannah decided to risk it. She reached out to pat the long, bony bit above the goat's rubbery muzzle. The goat snickered.

'She likes it!' Helen grinned with relief. She patted the goat too. Then she gave a squeal. The animal had dropped her head and was nosing into the pocket of Helen's jeans. She used her big front teeth and long tongue to pull out a boiled sweet. She snaffled it, wrapper and all. 'Hey!' Helen tried to catch hold of its rope collar.

'Too late!' Hannah cried. One gulp and the sweet was gone. Already she thought the goat was perfect; silky and brown, with those enormous clever eyes. 'Who's a good girl, then?' she cooed, showering her with pats and strokes.

Helen wasn't so sure. 'You wouldn't say that if it was *your* sweet.' She walked on.

The goat turned from Hannah and followed Helen.

'Go away, shoo! I don't have any more!' she lied. She kept her hands firmly in her pockets, guarding the two sweets she had left.

The clever goat came and nudged her from behind.

'Get this thing off me!' Helen complained. She turned and backed off down the slope. But she was grinning, and she soon softened. Out came another sweet. She paused to unwrap it. Snaffle! It was gone. Helen checked to see if her fingers were still all there.

She held up her third and final sweet, and the goat gobbled it down. Still hungry, she began to nibble at the studs on Helen's jeans. Helen tugged away, the goat refused to let go. 'You can't eat that!' She pulled hard. Suddenly the goat did let go. Helen sat with a thud in the long grass. She looked up at a wicked glint in the goat's eye.

Laughing, Hannah hauled her to her feet.

'Let's get out of here!' If they stayed much longer, Helen fully expected to be eaten alive. She headed for the nearest wall, closely pursued by the goat.

Hannah waited until her sister had climbed over the wall before she put an arm around the goat's neck and gave her a farewell hug. Then she followed Helen. 'Wouldn't that be good?' she said casually. She glanced back at the nosy goat, who was poking her head over the wall, following their every move.

'What would?'

'If we could have a *goat* at Home Farm!' Hannah was thrilled by the idea.

'No!' Helen was still brushing herself down and checking her bruises. 'I don't want a goat head-butting me all over the place!'

Hannah smiled. 'No, but *our* goat wouldn't head-butt us, would it?' She dreamed on as they walked down into the valley.

'That must have been Nancy, Fred Hunt's goat at High Hartwell,' the man in the village shop told them. He weighed out toffees from a jar on the shelf. 'Nancy eats anything, given half a chance. How are you liking Home Farm?' he asked. He seemed to know who the twins were.

'The roof leaks.' Helen counted out her money. 'A window's broken, and the water's brown.'

'A touch of do-it-yourself should soon put that right.' Luke Martin smiled and handed her the toffees. He was a short, round-faced man with a neat beard and not much hair on top of his head. 'Tell your mum and dad to give me a shout if they need a hand. I'll pop up any time, except Saturday afternoon.'

The twins promised to pass on the message.

'I can get my sister, Carrie, to mind the shop and I'll come to help with the DIY, but on Saturday cricket comes first!' He took Helen's money and gave her some change. 'By the way, does your dad play cricket?' he asked.

'I don't think so.' Hannah stood by the door on their way out.

'Tell him he does now,' Luke grinned. 'Doveton cricket team is a man short.' He stared, puzzled, at the twins, then shook his head. 'Like two peas in a pod, you two!'

Helen frowned. 'Hannah's got a dimple. I haven't.' Anyone could tell them apart once they knew that.

The door bell tinkled overhead as she shut the door. It seemed to be a signal for a flock of white doves. They rose from the grey slate roof of the shop and flew to the ground, gathering round the twins' feet, jostling and pecking at the ground. Then Luke came out and threw a handful of crumbs. The doves cooed and pecked.

'Cricket,' Luke reminded them, as he went back inside to serve a new customer. A stiff-looking old man with a clipped grey moustache marched his dog through the middle of the pecking doves, up the step into the shop.

Helen and Hannah sat down on a bench in the sun to watch the birds feed. They saw the man come out of the shop again. He studied the twins coldly as he tucked a loaf of bread under his arm.

'Bye, Mr Winter!' they heard Luke's pleasant voice call.

The man didn't reply. 'Come here, Puppy!' He called sternly to his long-haired terrier. The old dog creaked to his feet and plodded up to him. Mr Winter put him on a short lead and walked up to the twins. 'Shouldn't you be at school?' he inquired icily.

They blushed. 'We would be, except we've only just arrived in Doveton, and there's only two days of school left before the spring holiday,' Hannah explained. 'We don't have to start until after the break.'

'Hmm.' Mr Winter sniffed, as if moving house was no excuse for two able-bodied girls to miss even an hour's schooling. His face was the kind that creased easily. 'In my day, I would have expected you there in uniform, all present and correct, as soon as you arrived; not roaming the countryside when you ought to be in lessons!'

He went on his way, grey hair cut bristle-short at the back, his blue blazer fastened, gold buttons gleaming. Puppy trotted obediently behind.

Hannah stared at Helen.

'Take no notice.' Luke popped his head round the door. 'That's just Mr Winter!'

The twins took a deep breath. They felt as if they'd failed a test they didn't even know they were taking.

'He was headmaster of Doveton Junior School . . . oh, centuries ago!'

They sat counting their blessings. 'Thank heavens he's not there now!' Helen whispered. Doveton Junior was where they would be going to school.

'His bark is worse than his bite.' Luke scattered more crumbs for the birds and winked at them. 'Mr Cedric Winter!'

Cedric! The twins grinned at one another.

'Cricket,' he reminded them as he went back inside.

'Yeah, yeah!' they agreed. They liked Luke. As they jumped to their feet, the doves fluttered then settled. 'See you later!'

They headed off to the waterfront, where they paddled the morning away, fed the swans and ate ice-cream.

'Not bad!' Helen sighed. She wriggled her toes in the cold, clear water.

'What's not bad?' Hannah held out her last scrap of ice-cream cornet for a swan. It pecked it from her hand, its long neck snaking forward.

'Doveton . . . everything. We're going to like it here!'

'And Home Farm,' Hannah agreed.

'As long as Dad doesn't manage to make it all fall down!'

'I'm hungry,' Helen announced, leading the way back home.

Hannah agreed. They ran along the lakeside; two lean, brown-skinned figures. They followed the path that led by the big old farm at the water's edge. It had a peculiar grassy ramp up to a first floor hayloft, and three fat round chimneys that looked like funnels on a ship.

Lakeside Farm was what the twins called a real farm. There were sheep in the fields and hens in the farmyard. Right now, they could see the farmer out with his dog, striding into the hills to fetch some of his flock. The dog ran ahead, the farmer whistled, the dog crouched low. Another whistle; the dog streaked up the green hill.

'Steady, Ben, steady!' The old farmer growled an order.

The black and white sheepdog held to a straight line. One whistle from the farmer brought him to the left, another to the right. Soon the dog had bunched together six or seven sheep. He herded them towards the farmer. 'Good dog, Ben! Steady!' Yet another whistle sent the dog hurtling up the hillside on a second fetch.

'I bet Speckle was that good, once.' Hannah sighed. She still had the old dog collar hidden away inside her sleeping-bag at home. Meanwhile, Ben was on his way down with a new huddle of sheep.

When the farmer and his dog had finished their work, they headed straight for the twins.

'Yes?' the old man growled. He looked them up and down. 'What do you two want?'

'Nothing!' Helen stammered. She felt herself go hot. 'We were just watching your dog, that's all.'

The farmer went on staring. 'This is private land you're on.'

Something about his fierce gaze made them stammer all the more. 'We're sorry,' Hannah said, 'we didn't know. We're new here.'

'That's the path over there!' He waved a stout stick which he held in one hand. ' "Keep To The Footpath", it says on that notice there. Can't you read?'

Helen realised they'd strayed from the path to get a better view of the dog at work.

The farmer grunted and looked from one to the other. 'Twins?' He spoke in short jerks, with long gaps in between.

They nodded. Hannah spoke up. 'I'm Hannah Moore, and this is my sister, Helen. We've just moved in to Home Farm.'

'Home Farm, eh?' He nodded at Helen. 'Hannah, eh?'

'No, I'm Helen.'

He switched to Hannah. 'And Helen?'

'No, I'm . . . !' Hannah gave up. People were always mixing them up.

'Well, I'm John Fox, and this is Lakeside Farm, and it's all my property,' he said bluntly.

'How old is Ben?' Helen dared to ask. She was getting used to the old man's growling voice and gruff manner.

'Ben? Let's see, he'll be six. Yes, six in November.'

The dog sat to heel, but his tail wagged when he heard them mention his name.

'He's a brilliant sheepdog.' Hannah risked praising him.

The lines in the old man's face softened. 'You think so?'

'Really fantastic!' Helen agreed.

'You hear that, Ben?' John Fox stooped to pat the dog, then put the stern look back on his face. 'Well, I've no more time to waste standing here chatting to you two. I've work to do.' He sniffed. 'Come on, Ben.' He turned and strode off, with the dog trotting close behind.

Helen and Hannah breathed easily again. 'Do you

think all farmers are as unfriendly as Mr Fox?' Hannah muttered.

'He wasn't *that* bad!' Helen said slowly.

'Yes, he was. The dog was nice, though.'

'Yep, the dog was definitely nice.'

Quickly the twins took the track up the fell, past High Hartwell. They caught a glimpse of Nancy the goat in the thick of her field of buttercups. At last they reached Home Farm, in time to see the empty removal van inching its way out on to the narrow road.

Their dad stood at the gate. He gave them a wave. 'How was your morning?'

'Great! We met two nice animals and two horrible people!' Hannah flopped against the chestnut tree for a quick rest. Then she headed across the yard. 'I'm starving!'

'Typical!' he grinned. 'Your mum's driven over to Nesfield to put finishing touches to the cafe. Come inside and help me make a sandwich.'

They followed him. 'Cricket!' Hannah said with an air of mystery. She remembered they'd also met one nice person. She delivered Luke Martin's message to her dad.

'Not me, sunshine.' David Moore slapped slices of cheese between hunks of brown bread. 'I've hardly ever held a bat in my life!'

The twins told him this wouldn't make any difference to Mr Martin. 'Can we come and watch?' Helen asked.

'Over my dead body.'

'That means we can!' Hannah said with a laugh. As they helped to make lunch, they chatted on about Nancy the goat at High Hartwell, about Luke Martin's white doves and Ben the marvellous sheepdog – and all the sheep, cows and chickens they'd spotted during their morning's travels.

'Hey-up!' their dad said, raising his eyebrows suspiciously. 'Do I feel a request coming on?'

'No!' They both denied it, all wide-eyed and innocent. A silence grew. Hannah made her dad a cup of tea.

'Now I *know* you want something!' he joked.

'Well, it's just that we've been thinking . . .' Helen started off. She glanced at Hannah. The plan was to let the idea slip casually into the conversation.

Hannah cut in. 'Don't you think that what we need at Home Farm is a couple of nice friendly sheepdogs?

And maybe a cat or two?' She fancied an exact copy of the Ben type of dog; long-haired, floppy-eared, with a great white ruff of fur.

David Moore waved an arm round the kitchen. Boxes were piled high, there was a dripping tap, a door that wouldn't lock. 'No,' he said, 'what we need at Home Farm is some sets of good strong shelves, a plumber and a locksmith!'

Hannah and Helen's dream fell flat again. 'Does that mean we can't have dogs and cats?' Hannah asked quietly.

'Or goats, or fluffy yellow chicks, or black and white calves on wobbly legs?' Helen sounded hurt, trying to soften her dad's hard heart.

'No.'

'Just one small dog?' Hannah pleaded.

'No. You'll just have to wait.' He finished his sandwich and picked up a spanner from the table. Soon he was hard at work fixing the dripping tap.

The twins moped off into the yard. They found an old rope in the barn and slung it over a tree branch to make a swing.

' . . . A budgie?' Hannah pleaded when their dad came into the fresh air for a breather. His jeans were soaking wet after an accident with the plumbing system.

'No!' He went back inside.

' . . . A goldfish?' Helen suggested, as if it was the very least he could do.

'No!' he shouted from the kitchen.

'I think he means it.' Helen turned to Hannah.

They admitted defeat.

Three

'Right, you two!' Mary Moore came into the twins' bedroom early on their first Saturday morning at Home Farm. 'Come on, get a move on or we'll be late!'

'Why, where are we going?' Hannah stumbled into her clothes. Helen put on anything that came to hand; a striped red and white T-shirt and frayed denim shorts.

'Jumble sale!' their mum announced.

And, before they knew it, the whole family had gobbled a breakfast of toast and honey, and were swooping down the hill to a jumble sale at Doveton village hall.

Elbowing her way through the crowd, Mary Moore bought a pair of flowered curtains for a pound from Mrs Saunders.

'They're from a very good home!' Valerie Saunders whispered to Mary Moore. 'Mr Winter sent them in. That's him over there, on the electrical goods stall!'

The twins already knew who to avoid. They went in a wide circle round the old headmaster, leaving their mum to chat with Mrs Saunders. But their dad collared them and hauled them over to Mr Winter's stall.

'Uh-oh!' Helen cursed their luck.

'Here, give me a hand with this lot!' David Moore made them hold out their hands. He piled them high with old toasters, hair-dryers and half a hi-fi set without its speakers.

'They're from a very good home!' Mr Winter told him in a low, confidential voice. 'Mrs Saunders from Doveton Manor sent them in!'

'Well, I'm sure they'll come in useful!' Their dad paid the money and steered the twins through the jostling crowd.

'I can't see a thing!' Hannah complained. Someone trod on her toe. 'Ouch!'

'Me neither!' Helen barged into a stone pillar. The hi-fi wobbled.

'Watch where you're going!' David Moore warned.

'We would if we could!' they told him from behind their mass of jumble.

Then Luke Martin grabbed their dad. Before he knew it, he was sixth in the batting order for the village First Eleven.

'Two o'clock this afternoon,' Luke said.

The bargain-hungry crowd swallowed him before David had time to stutter out a refusal.

The twins smiled sweetly at him. 'Now, please can we take these things out to the car and then have twenty pence for orange-juice and a bun?' Helen asked.

Mr Moore forked out the money, but before the twins reached the refreshment table Hannah spotted another bargain. She went back to Mrs Saunders' stall and seized a chipped brown bowl.

'Why do we want that?' Helen frowned. Round the outside of the bowl she read the word 'DOG' in big black letters.

Hannah blew her fringe clear of her forehead. 'You never know. A dog bowl could be just what we need some day.'

'Where shall I put these?' Helen tramped through the door with the flowery curtains from the jumble. Hannah had already nipped upstairs to hide the old bowl.

'In the lounge. That's where they should fit best.' Her mum was busy trying out the second-hand toaster. 'I'll get your dad to fix a curtain rail.'

Helen and Hannah went off to the lounge and laid the curtains flat along the back of the sofa.

'I like this, it's a nice room.' Hannah vaulted over and bounced onto the soft cushions. There were wild roses in a jug on the windowsill, and the low beams gave the whole place a cosy feel.

'Things are looking up,' Helen agreed. They had proper beds in the bedroom, and the water in the taps had turned from brown to sparkling clear.

From the kitchen came the smells of scrubbed wood and things baking in the oven. Sunshine spilled in through the open door.

'What do you think?' The twins' dad came downstairs after lunch in a cricket sweater several sizes too big and a pair of crumpled, off-white trousers. He'd grabbed them on a stall at the jumble. 'Will I do?' he asked, giving a twirl.

'Fine,' their mum said firmly. She darted a warning look at the twins.

'I'm not sure if the black trainers match.' Hannah offered her opinion.

'Nit-picker!' David Moore looked out of the window. 'Anyway, they'll have to do. Here's Luke now.' He glanced round with a look of panic. 'Anyone fancy coming along to give me a bit of support?'

'You've changed your tune,' said Hannah.

'I wouldn't miss this for the world!' Helen whispered.

They sat high-up in the front of Luke Martin's delivery van, looking down at the cricket field just outside the village, on the one area of flat ground in the valley. Men in white had already gathered there to practise.

'Good luck!' the twins called, as their dad climbed down from the van.

'It looks as if I'll need it!' he said. He went nervously to join his team.

By the time the Doveton side went in to bat, Mary Moore had made friends with the cricket wives and Hannah and Helen were bored. It was a slow sort of game, they decided. They arranged to go off for a stroll.

'OK, but your dad will be batting soon,' their mum told them. 'Don't be too long.'

They agreed only to go as far as Lakeside Farm. 'We'll be back in time to see you bat,' they promised.

'Don't bother. I'll be out for a duck!'

Helen rolled her eyes. 'Out for a duck?' she muttered as they took the overgrown path towards the edge of the lake.

'Don't ask me,' Hannah shrugged.

Soon, the strange, round chimneys of Lakeside Farm came into view. There was no one in the fields today, just sheep grazing quietly. Perhaps everyone was at the cricket match, or shopping in Nesfield.

'I wonder where Ben is?' Helen said. They jumped from the path down a short bank on to the pebbly shore. She picked up a flat stone and tried to flick it so that it would skim across the surface of the water, bouncing as it went.

'It's probably his day off.' Hannah reckoned that even sheepdogs needed to rest. There was no sign of old John Fox, who'd told them to keep to the path.

For a while they threw stones, seeing who could get the most bounces.

'Four!' Helen claimed.

'Six!' Hannah sent one whizzing far out on to the lake.

They didn't spot Ben running along the shore towards them until he was almost there. His sharp, sudden bark made them jump. They spun round, dropping their handfuls of stones.

Ben barked again. He crouched low, barked sharply, jumped up and turned. He ran a few steps, stopped, barked and waited.

'What is it, boy?' Helen frowned.

The dog did the same thing over again, coming close, then leading them off. His long pink tongue lolled, his chest heaved in and out.

'It looks like he wants us to follow.' Hannah watched closely as he ran ahead. 'Come on, we'd better do as we're told!'

'What about the cricket?' Helen hesitated.

'This looks more important than a boring old cricket match!' It seemed as if Ben had run a long way to fetch them. 'Anyway, we won't go far.'

Helen nodded. 'OK, boy, you lead, we'll follow!'

The twins sprinted along the shore and up the bank. Ben guided them past the silent farm. A tractor stood in the yard, the doors of the house were shut tight. Hannah slowed down to see if there was any sign of the old farmer. Ben began to bark again; an impatient, urgent sound.

'Something's wrong!' Helen had a creepy feeling at the back of her neck. 'Come on, Hannah, we'd better get a move on. I'm sure Ben knows what he's doing!'

The dog ran on up the fell where they'd first seen him at work. He kept checking to see that they were following. They gasped and drew air into aching lungs as they struggled to keep up.

'Where's he taking us?' Hannah paused with a bad stitch in her side. They were heading for a rocky slope. A scree of loose stones lay ahead. Their feet would slide and slip. It began to look dangerous.

Ben barked even louder at them. He ran on to the scree and sent small stones slipping down. But he wouldn't let them give up now. He came back to Helen to lead her across the stones.

With pounding hearts, they followed. The flat stones crunched and slid underfoot. They were making for a block of big rocks on the summit. Shadows fell as they came near to the rocks. Ben bounded on to the top and stood looking down as they struggled after.

'Wait!' Helen caught Hannah by the arm. They were perched halfway up the final climb. 'Can you hear something?'

Hannah strained to hear. There was only the wind, and the sound of her own breathing.

'Listen!' Helen heard a small yelping cry. It came from somewhere beyond the tall rocks.

'Yes!' Hannah heard it too. 'Something's hurt or trapped! Come on!'

They climbed again, with Ben waiting on the summit. Hannah found a way up the final stretch. She hauled herself to the top and lay flat on her stomach, gasping. Over the other side, the rocks fell away into an old quarry. There was a drop of about twenty metres, a sheer cliff face.

Helen joined her. She gazed down into the big, scooped-out quarry. The sides were practically bare, the bottom covered in bushes and weeds, old barbed-wire, pieces of scrap metal. 'Over there!' She pointed to the coils of rusted wire. 'That's where the sound is coming from!'

The yelping was louder now. Ben barked and trotted along the ridge.

'How do we get down?' Hannah knew that whatever was down there needed help. She looked in all directions. There was no path, no easy way.

Helen began to crawl on all fours after the sheepdog. 'Ben will show us how to get down!' She gritted her teeth. She didn't like the height, or the wind catching at her as she crawled.

The dog seemed to understand. He picked his way along the ridge, found a way down that went in steps across the grey slate cliff face.

Helen glanced round at Hannah. 'Should we risk it?' There were small bushes to cling on to on the route he'd chosen, in case they slipped.

Hannah nodded. She couldn't bear the sound of the poor, hidden creature whining from the tangle of wire.

Slowly they inched their way down into the bottom of the quarry. The wind dropped to a dead calm. They crawled amongst damp shadows, looking for safe footholds, their hearts lurching as loose stones gave way.

Ben got there first. He looked up, knowing that his patience had been rewarded. He came up to them as their feet finally reached firm ground. Then he trotted to the tangle of wire and weeds. He nosed into it. The twins followed.

Helen crouched beside him. At first she could see only coarse grass and nettles. Hannah peered in from the other side. The whining came from right in the centre.

'There!' Hannah pointed to a pair of shining eyes. She leaned in and parted the grass. 'It's a puppy! It's caught in the barbed-wire, poor little thing!'

Four

'It can't move!' Hannah could see that the puppy's long black hair was caught up on the sharp spikes. It whimpered when it tried to move forward.

'Hang on, I'll get something to pull the wire away with!' Helen stood up and looked around. There was a long metal post propped against a boulder. She went to fetch it.

'Hurry!' Carefully Hannah reached in to stroke the dog. He watched her every move. His nose nuzzled against her hand. 'I think he's injured as well!' She could see small patches of sticky blood on the fur round his neck.

Helen used the post to bend back some of the coils of wire. She had to do it gently; the poor dog was tangled in it. Nettles stung her ankles and bare arms, but she went on trying to separate the strands of wire with the pole.

Soon Hannah was able to ease closer towards the puppy. She stroked his head, gently untwisted the knots of hair from the sharp spikes. 'Nearly!' she whispered. 'Just hang on for a few more minutes!'

Ben sat close by, his tongue flecked white, his ribs heaving.

'Good boy, Ben,' Helen said. 'It looks like you saved this pup's life!'

Ben waved his tail to and fro across the dusty ground.

At last Hannah managed to free the final tangle. 'Hold the wire back while I pull him out,' she whispered to Helen. Gently she slid both arms under the puppy's belly and eased him free. Then she laid him on a patch of grass.

He was only a few months old, not yet fully grown. His coat was dusty black along his back and to the white flash at the tip of his tail. His chest was white, his legs speckled grey. His big brown eyes closed as they knelt over him.

'Poor thing!' Helen was afraid that the rescue had come too late to save his life. He breathed in shallow gasps, unable to raise his head. 'I wonder how he got here?'

Hannah knew there was no time to think of that now. 'We have to get him out of here as fast as we can!' The dog wasn't heavy; he was skin and bone, and only half the size of sturdy Ben. But there was a difficult climb out of the quarry. She decided to lift him and make for the same route as before. 'Up here?' She turned to wait for Ben to show them the way.

The twins took it in turns to carry the injured puppy. One went ahead, checking each ledge and foothold, ready to take over the carrying. The puppy lay limp in their arms, hardly breathing. At last they reached the top.

They rested there, sitting in the sunshine, catching their breath.

Soon Ben was on his feet, urging them on, reminding them that they still needed to find help. They looked around, trying to get their bearings. The quarry was in the middle of nowhere. Which way should they go now?

Once more Ben took charge. He headed west towards the sinking sun. They marched after him through the ferns and heather, still taking turns to carry the rescued puppy. Eventually Ben led them to the edge of the rough ground, to a wall and a lane beyond.

Helen recognised it. 'This is our lane!' She pointed up the hill. Home Farm sat against the hillside, nestling beneath the huge chestnut tree. It was about a kilometre up the lane.

'Let's take him straight up there,' Hannah decided. 'He needs water. I don't think he can last much longer!'

'OK,' Helen agreed. 'Come on, Ben!' She called the sheepdog to go with them.

But Ben knew his job was done. He gave one bark, then turned and headed downhill towards Lakeside Farm. He didn't look back, just trotted home, where he knew he would soon be missed.

They half-ran the final stretch alone. There was no one at Home Farm. They would have to nurse the puppy and clean his wounds by themselves.

They reached the house and went quickly inside. 'Put him down on the rug,' Helen suggested. She held the kitchen door open, then ran upstairs to fetch a blanket. She wrapped it round the shivering creature.

Hannah fetched the jumble sale dish and filled it with water. She knew it would come in useful one day. The puppy was still too weak to lift his head to drink. He lay there, eyes closed. She looked up. 'I think he's going to die!'

'No!' Helen ran to the drawer where they kept knives and forks. She found a bundle of drinking-straws and brought one back. Bending down to the dish, she drew water into the straw. Then she put her finger over the top end. The water stayed in the straw. She asked Hannah to tilt the puppy's head up and back. Hannah eased his lips apart with her free hand. Then Helen pushed the straw into his mouth. She let the water trickle out.

They watched the puppy blink and swallow. Hannah stroked his throat. 'Do it again, Helen, I think it's working!' There was a tiny gleam in his eyes as they opened and looked back at her.

Helen did it all over again. This time the puppy took a bigger swallow. Less of the water dribbled out of the side of his mouth. Now he managed to raise his head and give one faint wag of his tail.

'See, he's going to be all right!' Helen breathed.

They had tears in their eyes as they brought the puppy back to life. Before long, they had him lapping water for himself. He was still too weak to stand, so they kept him carefully wrapped in the blanket. They propped his head on a cushion, then bathed his wounds with disinfectant and warm water.

'Shall we give him something to eat?' Helen asked after they'd made him clean and comfortable.

'Not yet.' Hannah had an idea that all he wanted to do now was sleep. He licked her hand with his pink tongue. She tucked the blanket under him. 'He hasn't got a collar,' she pointed out. 'I wonder who he belongs to?'

'Maybe no one. He could be a stray.'

'Or just lost?'

They gazed at him as he settled down to sleep. 'If he was only lost, he'd be wearing a collar,' Helen said. *Oh, I want him to be a stray!* she thought. *Then we might be allowed to keep him* . . . Her thoughts raced ahead. 'I bet somebody abandoned him!' she whispered.

Hannah ran one hand through her dark fringe,

pushing it back from her forehead. 'What? You mean somebody just threw him in the quarry to get rid of him?' She couldn't believe that people could be so cruel.

Even Helen backed off from this idea. 'Not threw exactly. More like, they left him on the mountain to fend for himself, and he just wandered to the quarry and fell in somehow!'

Just then, their guesswork was cut short. There was the sound of a car engine struggling up the hill. It was Luke Martin in his van, bringing their mum and dad home from the cricket.

'Oh no, the cricket!' Hannah shot to the window. She'd forgotten all about where they were supposed to be.

Helen joined her. On the rug behind them, snug under a blanket, the rescued puppy slept soundly.

'What'll they say?' Hannah gasped.

'About the cricket?'

'No, about Speckle.' Hannah gave him a name. He wasn't just 'the puppy', not now they'd saved his life. His legs were speckled grey and white so the name fitted him, and it just popped out of her mouth as the van drew into the farmyard.

They ran out as their mum and dad stood waving goodbye to Luke Martin. David Moore had a smile from ear to ear. He turned and spotted them.

'Where were you?' he cried. 'You missed a treat!'

'More to the point, what *did* happen to you two?' their mum insisted. 'Didn't you say you'd be back to watch the cricket? I was getting worried.'

'You needn't have,' Helen said. 'See, we're OK!'

'Yes, I knew you'd get bored,' their dad agreed. 'You should've stayed though! I was hitting the ball all over the place!' He was too excited to wonder where the twins had been.

They hung back in the farmyard and looked at one another. Who was going to be the one to tell their news?

'He got twenty-five runs,' their mum said. 'Now there'll be absolutely no stopping him!' She slipped indoors with a quiet shake of her head.

Their father blew on his fingernails and polished them against his chest. 'It was nothing. Beginner's luck, that's all!'

They couldn't get a word in edgeways. Then it was too late. They had to follow their mum and dad into the kitchen in silence.

Hannah stared at Helen. 'What on earth will they say?' she whispered.

'When they see Speckle?'

'Fast asleep . . .'

' . . . On our kitchen rug?'

Five

'You can call him Speckle for now.' Mary Moore took it calmly. She'd got over her surprise at seeing the dog wrapped in the blanket, and listened quietly to the twins' excited tale. 'It sounds like Ben from the farm did a fantastic job. And you were both brilliant to help rescue the puppy like that. But you realise that as soon as he gets better we'll have to find out where he came from and give him back.' She nodded firmly, then went upstairs to get changed.

'Your mum's right,' David Moore said. 'The owner's probably worried sick about him. We must do all we can to find out where he belongs.'

Hannah and Helen couldn't believe their ears.

'Doesn't rescuing Speckle mean anything?' Hannah pleaded. 'He would have died without us!'

'Don't we have the right to look after him now?' Helen wanted to nurse him. 'We want to take care of him forever!'

After all, if there was an owner, it was a careless one. They knew they would make much better owners. They would feed him, and train him, and take him for walks.

'That's just not possible,' their dad said gently. 'I'll tell you what, though.' He wanted to cheer them up. 'Your mum's right; it sounds as if old Ben did a great job, leading you to Speckle in the first place!'

Hannah hung her head, Helen fiddled with the bent straw. She still held it, twisting it until it tore in two. Meanwhile, Speckle slept on.

Their dad scratched his chin and ruffled his wavy hair. He went to study Speckle, whose head poked out of the red checked blanket. He looked up at the twins. 'I know what you're thinking,' he said quietly.

'What?' They could both feel the hot tears stinging the insides of their eyelids.

'You're thinking that we're saying we have to find

out who owns him because we don't want a dog in the first place.' His voice was calm and kind.

Hannah nodded. 'You don't care what happens to Speckle.'

'You don't like dogs. You don't like animals.' Helen was upset and didn't think before she spoke.

He stood up and thought about this. 'No, you're wrong. I had a dog myself when I was a kid.'

Hannah glanced up. 'You did?'

'Scraps. He was a mongrel. I took him everywhere with me. I loved that dog.'

'Well then!' Hannah said.

Her dad put an arm round her shoulder. 'So I know how much time they take up looking after them properly. You can't just get a puppy because he looks cute and plays with toilet rolls, like they do on telly!'

She gave a small smile.

'They need someone to train them, and they need space to run around, and . . .' He slowed to a stop. Helen had flung open the kitchen door and was pointing to the open fields. 'OK,' he admitted, 'we've got the space, and I'm not saying we're against having pets at Home Farm in the future. But the fact remains that Speckle must have an owner somewhere, and . . .'

'Maybe not. Maybe he's a stray!' Helen jumped in with her own theory. 'He wasn't wearing a collar!'

'It's possible, I suppose. But we don't know for sure,' he pointed out.

Their mum came back downstairs in a clean white shirt. She rubbed cream into her hands. 'I must say, I did wonder about that,' she admitted.

'What?' Hannah was quick to take her up.

'Why he wasn't wearing a collar. And why he was out there, miles from anywhere. He's a very young dog to be out by himself. You'd expect someone to take more care.'

The twins allowed their hopes to flicker back into life. Helen crossed her fingers, Hannah closed her eyes.

Their mum stooped over the huddle of skin and bones inside the blanket. 'I wonder how long you'd been stuck in that quarry before Ben found you,' she murmured.

Just then Speckle woke up. He turned his head to lick her fingers.

'Someone's going soft!' David Moore winked at them. 'I think she likes him!'

'I'm not! And I never said I didn't.' She put her head

to one side.

'Mum . . .' Helen came up with her best argument. Speckle's whole future was at stake. 'You know how you're always coming home with things you've rescued?' Their mum was famous for collecting junk that no one else wanted. Their dad called her Magpie.

'*Objects*, yes,' she admitted. She could never pass by a builders' skip or a car-boot sale without taking a peep.

'And you never bother to try and find out where *they* come from, do you?'

'No. But that's because someone's finished with them and thrown them out. And besides, they're objects, not living things!' She was beginning to smile at Helen.

'It's the same!'

'No, it's not. We don't know that Speckle's owner threw him out, do we? What if he belongs to someone in the village? What would you do if you looked after him and called him your own, then one day you were walking down the main street and oops, you bumped straight into the real owner? What then?'

Helen clamped her mouth shut.

'No!' Hannah jumped in with a good reason why her mum might be wrong. 'If Speckle has got an owner, they'll put one of those adverts in the paper. You know, "Lost, One Puppy . . ."!'

'Yes!' Helen saw what she meant. 'So, if no one is actually looking for him, that must prove he's a stray!'

'Maybe.' Mary Moore thought long and hard. 'But I still think we should make an effort to look for his owner ourselves.'

'Listen,' their dad said, 'the puppy's luck was in when you two went to rescue him, we know that.

And we're proud of you. So why not spoil him to death while you get the chance? Enjoy having him here as a sort of lodger, then, when he has to go home, maybe you can go and visit him. How's that?'

For now they had to agree.

'Right, where shall we start?' Their dad became brisk. 'First off, we should call Sally Freeman to check his cuts and bruises.' Sally was a vet they'd met at the cricket match earlier in the day. 'Second, let's find out what he likes to eat. Third, I think we should drop in at Lakeside Farm and talk to old John Fox about Ben's part in all this.' He paused. 'Who knows, the puppy might even belong to the farm. If not, Mr Fox will have heard of any farmer round here who's lost one. In a small place like Doveton, everyone knows everyone else's business.'

Mary Moore agreed. 'We'll do it first thing tomorrow.'

Sally Freeman came up to Home Farm that evening. She was a tall woman with long, blonde hair tied back from her face.

She examined Speckle and gave him the all-clear. 'Apart from the cuts from the barbed-wire, of course, and the malnutrition.' She felt carefully along the puppy's ribs. 'You don't often see one as bad as this. He's bound to be very weak.' She decided to give Speckle an injection and told them exactly what he should eat. 'He'll be fine soon,' she assured them. She closed her bag and prepared to leave. 'He's a very lucky dog. You two came along in the nick of time.'

Mary showed her to the door. 'I'll look out for anyone who's lost a Border collie pup,' she promised. 'Don't worry, we'll soon have the little chap safely back where he belongs!'

We hope not! Helen and Hannah stood side by side, saying nothing. They spent the rest of the evening close by Speckle's side.

Soon there would be people on the farms, and all round Doveton village, trying to find Speckle's proper owner. And all they wanted was for him to stay with them in their new, perfect-for-pets set-up, at Home Farm.

Six

Next day, David Moore rang John Fox to ask him up for a chat about a stray dog.

The farmer arrived in his grey Land-Rover. Ben sat next to him, looking down into the empty farmyard as they pulled up.

'Now then, what's this?' Mr Fox spotted the twins hanging about in the kitchen doorway, next to a stone trough full of geraniums that their mum had just planted.

Helen flicked a bee away from her face and frowned. She decided again that Mr Fox was hard to like. He was sharp and skinny, with a pointed nose and chin. His voice was a kind of snappy bark.

'Is your dad in?' He frowned back, glancing up at the mended window, then down at the bright red flowers.

Hannah stopped making a fuss of Ben. 'I'll go and get him,' she said quietly.

'Now then,' John Fox said again, when the twins' mum appeared from the old barn. 'You'll be Missus Moore?' He shook hands. He wore his grey jacket buttoned up, and a checked shirt, with a mustard yellow tie.

'Would you like to come in and look at the dog?' Mary Moore offered. She led them into the kitchen.

'It's a stray, you say?' John Fox glanced at Speckle, who was stretched out on his blanket in the corner of the room. 'My!' He shook his head. 'He could do with a good feed!'

Now Ben wagged his tail and went quietly to say hello. He sniffed at Speckle's disinfected cuts. Speckle lifted himself on to his wobbly legs and wagged his own tail feebly.

Helen watched the two of them making friends. 'Does Speckle belong to you?' she asked the farmer, dreading the answer 'yes'.

He shook his grey head. 'No, I'd never treat any dog of mine like that!'

Speckle's ribs showed; there wasn't a scrap of flesh on him. Still, he looked better than when they'd first seen him.

Helen heaved a sigh of relief. 'We found him in the old quarry. Ben took us there.' She explained how the dog had taken them to the spot where the puppy lay trapped.

The old farmer grunted. 'That's where you'd got to, was it?' He gave his own dog a pat on the sturdy side. 'Good lad, Ben.' He sounded proud, explaining that he'd been to town and come home to find Ben missing. He'd turned up at last. 'Worn out, he was,' Mr Fox said. 'I wondered what he'd been up to.'

Just then, Hannah came back with her dad. She'd found him in the attic, fixing up a darkroom for his photography work. He smelt of chemicals. The two men shook hands.

Helen sidled up to her sister. 'Speckle doesn't belong to Mr Fox!' she beamed.

Hannah bit her lip. 'Good!' she whispered.

'It's still a mystery then,' their dad said, listening

to their neighbour. 'We're no nearer to knowing where Speckle came from.'

'I'd like to know why you call him that.' John Fox rubbed his stubbly chin. He watched carefully, as the stray dog settled back on to his blanket, worn out by Ben's lively greeting.

They turned to Hannah for an answer. She blushed. 'It's his legs,' she said. 'They're covered in grey speckles. And I found an old collar,' she admitted. 'It was hanging on the back of the door. It says "Speckle" on the name tag. That's what made me think of the name in the first place.'

The farmer grunted again. 'Aye, I knew the Speckle that lived here before. He was a fine dog. A champion. It made me wonder to hear you call this one by the same name.'

Mary Moore smiled. 'Why not fetch the collar, Hannah, and let us see it? Maybe it'll fit this Speckle!'

Hannah went to her bedroom. She brought the leather strap with the metal disc, which was smooth and cold, and lay pressed into her palm. She only half-wanted to try the collar on Speckle. It was like Cinderella and the glass slipper; if it fitted, she knew she would want to keep him for good. She handed it to Helen.

Helen fastened it in its tightest hole. 'It fits!'

Hannah breathed out.

'Doesn't he look sweet?' Helen laughed at him. The collar meant that he didn't look like a stray any longer; more like he belonged.

David Moore turned to their visitor. 'Sorry to drag you up here for nothing.'

'Nay, I don't mind. But it makes me mad to think of folks treating their animals this way.'

Helen and Hannah warmed to him. 'Tell us about old Speckle, Mr Fox,' Helen said, as her mum handed him a cup of tea and a biscuit.

'Ah now, *there* was a dog!' He sat at the table and dipped his biscuit in his tea. 'He *was* a champion. He won ribbons at Doveton Trials, then he went on to win them for the whole of the Lakes! You should've seen him!' He shook his head at the memory.

'I wish we had!' Hannah agreed.

'You've never seen a dog like that one for a fetch. Straight as an arrow up the fell. Rounded them up, penned them like magic. You hardly needed to tell him what to do, he knew it all himself!' The old farmer sounded as if he could still see him streaking across the hills; the white flash of his tail, the long, loping stride. Absent-mindedly he dropped Ben a corner of his biscuit. The dog waited obediently. 'Here, Ben!' Then he darted to the chair to snaffle the crumbs.

'What about *our* Speckle? Would he make a champion sheepdog?' Hannah asked. Mr Fox seemed to be the expert.

The old man laughed; somewhere between a bark and a cough. 'Nay, he's a townie, that one. He doesn't have the farm look.'

'How can you tell?'

'I can, that's all. He's not been bred as a working dog, I can tell you that much.'

Hannah screwed her mouth up tight. 'I bet he could learn.'

'Nay, you've to breed them as champions,' he insisted. 'Like Ben here.' The dog's tail wagged at the sound of his name.

Helen drew Hannah off to Speckle's corner. 'He's only saying that! I reckon we could train Speckle to be a really good sheepdog!'

'Yes, we'd soon get him to do as he was told!'

Hannah felt she would love to try.

'If they gave us the chance!' Helen muttered.

'We could get him to sit and stay, and come, and do everything perfectly!'

They plotted and planned what they would do if they were allowed to keep the puppy.

'Well, I guess we'll never know.' Their dad cleared the table after the grown-ups had finished their tea. 'We aim to find the owner,' he explained to the farmer. 'If you do hear of anyone who's lost a pup, will you let us know?'

They went into the yard, Ben trotting neatly at Mr Fox's heels.

The twins stayed behind. 'You know,' Helen told Hannah, 'the best thing for us to do is try our hardest to find out who Speckle belongs to, like Dad says.'

Hannah turned on her. 'How can you say that?'

'No, listen. We could take photos of him with Dad's camera, and stick them up in the shop in the village, and in Nesfield as well. Mum can have one for The Curlew. You know, a photo with a notice underneath; "Found, one Border collie . . ." '

Helen was shocked. 'You sound as if you can't wait to get rid of him!'

'No, I want to keep him just as much as you! But Mum and Dad mean it; they want us to find the real owners. So let's get it over and done with.' She felt herself torn in two, between longing to keep Speckle and the fear of having to give him back. Better to get moving than to sit back hoping it would never happen.

Hannah sighed. Then another thought struck her. 'You know, Helen, if we *did* find the owner, maybe they would let us keep Speckle after all?'

'You mean, we could persuade them to let him stay at Home Farm?' Helen caught a glimmer of new hope. Her eyes lit up. 'You never know!' she nodded.

'Right, so we'll take these portraits of Speckle. We'll ask Dad to help us develop them. Then tomorrow we can put one in Luke Martin's shop window and take them round to see if anyone recognises him.'

'OK.' Hannah turned away and went to wash the teacups. She felt they were doing the right thing at last. 'But suppose we don't get anywhere? What if no one recognises him?'

'Then,' Helen darted a quick look out of the window. Mr Fox's old Land Rover was pulling out of the yard. She held up two pairs of crossed fingers for Hannah to see. 'Who knows?'

'Good idea!' David Moore was only too glad to help. 'You can get a couple of nice close-up shots of his head, and some full-length shots!'

Their mum praised them for being sensible and doing what was best for Speckle. She promised to take some photos into Nesfield. 'I'll stick some in the window at The Curlew,' she said.

So they spent Sunday evening taking photographs of Speckle. He squirmed and wriggled and when they

pointed the camera lens at him, he crept off his blanket. Once he came up and licked the camera. They used a whole film and got close-up views, side views, full-length shots of him sitting, standing and wriggling.

They took the film straight up to their dad's new attic dark-room. The window was blacked out with dark fabric and tape. The hot little room smelled of developing-chemicals. They worked in a special dim red light that didn't ruin the pictures as they developed them.

Soon the roll of film was hanging up to dry. Then they could choose and print the best shots. Each shape came up on the stiff paper; grey shadows at first, turning magically into beautiful black and white portraits of adorable Speckle. His eyes looked huge, his head was cocked to one side in one, his tongue half-out in the next. Hannah lifted each print out of the tray and hung it up to dry. Helen chose the next negative, and they began the process all over again.

At last they decided that they'd had enough. David Moore switched off the special lamps and opened the attic door. 'That's it for now,' he said.

'Suppertime!' their mum called upstairs.

The twins ran down to show her their pictures. Speckle came to the bottom of the stairs to greet them.

'Look, he's getting stronger!' Helen stroked and fussed him. 'He'll soon be able to play out in the yard!'

'One step at a time,' Mary Moore reminded them. She laughed as Speckle tangled himself up between the legs of the kitchen chairs. 'Put him back on his blanket,' she told Hannah.

Hannah put him out of harm's way. 'Stay!' she said, as sternly as she could.

He trotted towards the table.

She put him back again. 'Stay!' She turned to go and eat her home-made pizza. She felt the puppy's tail tickle her legs.

Her dad laughed. 'That's a champion sheepdog you've got there; very obedient!'

Hannah gave in. She let Speckle crawl under her chair. He waited for scraps to fall his way. 'Mr Fox said he needed feeding up!' she protested.

'You'd better get those notices ready before you go to bed,' their mum advised. 'I'll take them into town with me tomorrow.'

Helen and Hannah promised they'd be ready.

After supper, they cleared the table and set out card, scissors, glue and the photos. They used their best handwriting and a new set of felt-tipped pens. Speckle was allowed up on to a chair to sit and watch.

First, Hannah stuck a photo of Speckle on to each square of white card. She ruled a bright pink frame round the edges. Underneath, Helen wrote in bold capital letters:

Found!

male Border Collie puppy
9 months old, black and
white with grey speckled
legs, no collar.
phone Doveton 60294

Proudly she held up the finished card. 'What do you think?'

'Great!' Hannah was pleased with the result. She studied the photograph and sighed. 'I wonder where you come from!' she whispered longingly. 'And I wonder where on earth you're going to end up!'

Seven

'Speckle!'

'Speckle, put that down!'

'Speckle, come here, you naughty dog!'

'Helen, Hannah, help! The dog's nicked my trainer!'

Speckle had soon made himself at home at the farm. He put on weight and got into mischief, just like any nine month old puppy.

Every few minutes, a cry would go up, and there would be Mr Moore chasing the puppy across the kitchen out into the farmyard, one shoe on, one shoe off.

Or Speckle's little black and white face would appear round the bathroom door while Helen was brushing her teeth. He would shove the door, lose his balance and skid across the shiny floor.

Or else Hannah would be helping to put finishing touches to a tray of buns for her mum's cafe. Speckle's nose would come snuffling under her elbow. She would take him down from the chair and sound cross. 'No, Speckle, these aren't for you!' It was almost impossible not to give in to the melting brown eyes and wagging tail.

Dozens of 'Found' cards and photographs went round the village and into the shops and cafes in nearby Nesfield. John Fox even stuck a notice in the window of his Land-Rover. 'We'll get to the bottom of this,' he promised. The twins felt that he would like to wring the neck of the puppy's owner if ever they found him or her.

These days, during the spring holiday, they often made their way down to Lakeside Farm. Speckle was fit enough to come with them. Ben and he were firm friends, and though Mr Fox sometimes pretended to be too busy to chat, the twins thought that he didn't really mind them dropping in.

One day, almost a week after they'd rescued Speckle, with still no replies to their smart notices, they bumped into the old farmer and his dog outside Luke Martin's shop in Doveton. Speckle spotted Ben and raced through the flock of pecking doves to meet him.

'Now then!' John Fox made his usual greeting. 'You've still got the puppy, I see?'

Hannah smiled. 'Yes, and we haven't had a single phone call about him so far!' At first, she and Helen had jumped every time the phone rang. They'd held their breaths and crossed their fingers, hoping that it wouldn't be about Speckle. Now though, they were beginning to relax.

'We don't think anyone wants him back,' Helen told the farmer.

'What then?' He cast them a shrewd look.

Helen blushed and went vague. 'Mmm, we're not sure yet.'

'We haven't talked about it,' Hannah said. She tried to stop Speckle chasing the doves.

'But I'll bet you're wanting to keep him at Home Farm?' He ordered Ben into the car.

Helen and Hannah nodded. 'If Mum and Dad will let us.'

'I'd have him myself,' the farmer added. 'Only, he's not a farm dog, like I said.' He climbed up after Ben. Then he noticed Mr Winter heading down the street with Puppy. 'Watch out, here comes trouble,' he warned. 'Keep that pup on a lead!'

But it was too late. Speckle had seen Puppy. Ears flapping, tail wagging, all legs and bounce, he headed for the terrier.

The doves fluttered and scattered, Puppy growled, Speckle flew at him.

'I say!' Mr Winter pulled smartly at Puppy's lead. Speckle yapped and climbed all over him. 'Get down, you young ruffian! Get down, I say!' The old schoolteacher was in a fury. His grey eyes glared, his moustache quivered. 'You two girls, come right over here and restrain your animal!' There was a flurry of barking, yelping black and white fur.

John Fox winked at the twins.

Hannah ran to pull Speckle away. She seized him and he rolled into her arms, a mass of wriggling soft fur, hot breath and pink tongue.

Mr Winter pulled Puppy to heel. The dog looked miserable, his owner looked grim. 'I say!' He smoothed his blue blazer and tugged at his cuffs. Then he delivered his verdict on poor, over-friendly Speckle. 'The sooner that little savage is returned to his proper owner, the better!' he declared.

Hannah frowned and took him a safe distance away. Mr Martin, who had heard the commotion, came on to the step. 'Good morning, Mr Winter,' he said cheerfully.

The ex-headmaster gave him a frosty stare. He marched on, past a silent trio of Helen, Hannah and Speckle.

'Does everyone think that Speckle's a little savage?' Helen asked the farmer.

'Take no notice,' Mr Fox mumbled under his breath. 'He makes life misery for that little dog of his. He doesn't understand animals, not the least little bit. Of course, he's spent most of his life behind a desk!' He shook his head, started his engine and drove off.

The twins felt better. But Mr Winter struck again. He turned in the shop doorway. 'If you ask me, some people simply aren't fit to keep pets!' he announced. It was obvious he meant them.

Hurt by his words, Helen and Hannah headed for home. Even seeing Nancy the goat peering over her wall at them from her field halfway up the hill didn't cheer them up as much as usual.

The goat, of course, was looking for something to eat. Helen scratched her head and found her some sweet clover grass growing out of reach by the far side of the road. The goat snatched it from her hand and chewed greedily. Speckle sat patiently, tired by the excitement of his meeting with Puppy.

Hannah looked down at him. 'It's OK looking all sweet and innocent now!' she scolded.

He cocked his head to one side. Nancy gently butted Helen's shoulder. The clover was good; she wanted more. Helen obliged, and soon she was chewing on her second clump.

'Come on,' Hannah said at last, 'we promised to be back in time to help Dad get organised for his cricket match tonight.'

They set off up the hill, with Nancy braying longingly after them.

'Who's that?' Helen said as the farm came into view. 'Are we expecting visitors?'

Hannah shook her head and followed her sister's stare. There was a small green van parked outside the house.

They went through the gate, and Hannah let Speckle off the lead to scamper amongst weeds and old farm machinery in a far corner. They saw that one of the van doors was swinging open, and a man was standing talking to their dad.

Helen and Hannah felt a twinge of alarm. What did the stranger want? Helen pulled herself together first. It could be about anything. It didn't have to be something to do with Speckle.

David Moore nodded his head. He looked serious.

'Let's see what this is about!' Helen ran on. She'd already decided she didn't like the look of the stocky man at the door. He had very short, clipped, brown hair, and a thick neck and broad shoulders. He was dressed in a tight white T-shirt and jeans. It seemed he was talking at their dad, who could only nod and listen.

'. . . I saw the advert this morning.' The man spoke in a loud voice. 'I came straight over to Doveton and asked around. There was an old man walking down the main street with his dog. He told me I should come up here and ask about Prince.'

Helen stopped in her tracks. She turned to Hannah. The man had come looking for his puppy.

Panic gripped them, the loud voice pushed on.

'I live in Nesfield, but I was over here a couple of weeks ago with the dog. I was fishing by the lake. Prince ran off when I wasn't looking. I looked everywhere for him. In the end, I gave up. I thought he must have drowned or got run over. I went home without him. Then I saw the advert in the cafe window this morning, like I said.'

It sounded horribly true. The twins could hardly breathe from shock. This man had come to take Speckle away from them. Not knowing what was wrong, the puppy ran in and out of the old tractor wheels, chasing his own tail.

'What day were you fishing?' Their dad checked the story.

'Let's see. Not this week just gone. The week before. It would be the Tuesday.' He sniffed and looked round, catching sight of Hannah and Helen standing there white-faced and silent.

'Helen, Hannah, this is Danny Jones.' Their dad spoke quietly to them. 'He's come to take a look at Speckle.'

At first the twins didn't react.

'Mr Jones has lost a puppy somewhere round here.

He thinks it may be Speckle.'

'Prince.' Danny Jones corrected him.

'Where is he?' Mr Moore had his calm voice on, the one he used when he had to do something he didn't like. 'Can you fetch him please.'

They went off together, their legs feeling like lead, their mouths dry. This was what they had dreaded. Helen called in a faint voice, 'Here, Speckle!' She couldn't bear to call him Prince. He'd vanished amongst the nettles and dandelions.

They could hear their dad still checking their visitor's story. 'You say you live in town?'

'On the High Street. Look, I haven't got time to mess about.' He reached into his back pocket and unfolded a piece of paper. 'I brought this with me as proof. It's a receipt from the pet shop where I bought the dog. Proof that I'm the owner, see!'

David Moore studied the bill.

'I paid fifty pounds for that dog!' Danny Jones claimed, his temper rising. 'Now, will you lot just stop messing about and hand him over!'

By this time, the twins had managed to corner Speckle against the wall. He thought it was another game and darted out between Helen's legs, then whirled around and jumped up at her. She caught him. 'Come on, boy!' She hugged him close to her and carried him across the yard.

Hannah hung back by the old tractor. She couldn't bear to follow.

'You'd better take a look first,' David Moore pointed out to the stranger. 'Just in case it isn't the same dog.'

Danny Jones could see Speckle wriggling in Helen's arms. 'That's him,' he said in a flat voice. 'Now hand him over, will you?'

Speckle saw the man for the first time. Helen felt him stiffen. It must have been Jones's harsh voice, or the way he stood, legs wide apart, arms folded. The dog didn't like him. He bared his teeth and growled.

Hannah raced across the yard. 'How do you know it's him?' she demanded. 'You haven't even looked properly!' She was desperate to prove him wrong. 'What colour are his legs?' The way Helen had hold of him, his legs were hidden from view.

'Grey speckled,' Danny Jones said, his eyes narrowed, his voice sneering.

He could have seen that on the photo in the cafe, she realised too late. It didn't prove anything.

'Calm down, Hannah,' her dad said. He turned to Jones. 'You're sure?'

'Sure I'm sure. What is this, the third degree? Look, you saw the receipt. I told you the full story. He's always wandering off, the stupid dog. This time he went too far. He must've fallen into this quarry you told me about. I wouldn't hear him barking from down by the lake, would I?'

Slowly Mr Moore had to agree. He sighed. 'That's it then, girls. Give Speckle to me. I'll put him in the van.'

Helen was almost in tears, but she wouldn't let

herself down in front of the visitor. Only, she wished with all her heart that Danny Jones was a nicer, kinder, gentler man than he seemed, standing there demanding his dog. Prince was a terrible name, anyway, for the playful, affectionate puppy.

As her dad took him from her, Speckle wriggled and slipped to the ground. He seemed to know what was going on; that this man would take him away in the green van. It was clear that he didn't want to go. He ran growling across the yard.

Danny Jones slammed his car door and charged after him. Mr Moore held the twins back. Jones cornered Speckle by the trough of geraniums. He growled and bared his teeth; a tiny dog against a huge man. Jones moved in on him, arms spread wide, crouching low.

'You stay there, you little devil!' There was sweat trickling down his forehead, his voice was hard. He swore at the puppy.

'Dad!' Helen appealed. This was terrible. Speckle didn't want to go. Even if Danny Jones was the proper owner, Speckle would never be happy with him.

David Moore shook his head. 'Sorry, girls!'

Hannah closed her eyes. She didn't want to see the man close in on Speckle. He was down on one knee, speaking roughly. Speckle barked, the hair all along his spine stood on end. Jones meant to take him away. And there wasn't a thing they could do to help.

Speckle waited for Danny Jones to pounce. As the heavy man threw himself forward, the dog slid underneath. Jones landed with a crunch on the doorstep. Speckle ran free!

Eight

'Stop him!' Jones shouted and scrambled to his feet.

Speckle ran wide of Helen, Hannah and their dad. He headed for the open gate without looking back.

'Speckle!' Mr Moore made a move to follow. Neither of the twins went after him. They watched the white tip of the puppy's tail disappear through the gate. Only then did they give chase, knowing that he could easily outrun them all.

Danny Jones was the first to reach the gate and look up and down the lane. 'Where is he? Where did he go?' He was furious. 'You did that on purpose!' he yelled. 'You let him get away!'

They looked high and low. They went up the lane, calling out for the runaway puppy, searching amongst the bushes, over the walls, across the fields towards the rocky summit of the fell. There was no sign of the dog.

'He can't have vanished into thin air!' Danny Jones looked as if he would explode.

'No, but he could be well away by now,' David Moore pointed out. They'd been searching for about half an hour and their track had brought them full-circle, back to Home Farm.

'It's your fault!' Jones rounded on the twins. 'You let him go!'

They stared back, half-glad, half-afraid.

Their dad stepped in. 'It's not our fault that he resisted arrest!'

Jones shook his head angrily. 'Well, listen here, I'm off now.' He frowned at them. 'I have to meet someone in town.' He drew his van keys out of his pocket and pointed them towards Hannah and Helen. 'I can't mess around here any more. But it's Saturday tomorrow, and I'll be back. I'll turn the place inside out to find my dog!'

David Moore warned the twins not to say anything. 'OK, Mr Jones, we'll keep a lookout for him as well. Between us, we should be able to track him down.'

So Jones went off empty-handed. He revved his van engine and sped away. Somewhere on the hillside, Speckle lay hiding. Would he come home to the farm when he heard the van drive off? Or would he stay out all night, too scared to return? Would the twins ever see him again?

Questions jangled inside their heads as their dad told them to come inside. 'Time for a cuppa and a good long think,' he insisted.

Hannah felt she would burst. 'But, Dad, you don't believe he's telling the truth, do you?' Something told her that Jones wasn't genuine. And she couldn't forgive him for trying to grab Speckle and carry him off by force.

'I'm afraid I do.' David Moore sighed. 'Why would he make up the story about the fishing trip?'

'But he's so . . . awful!' Words failed Helen. She too would hate to see Speckle sent off with this stranger.

'Yes, but just because you two don't like him

doesn't mean to say he can't take his dog home,' their dad pointed out.

'But Speckle doesn't like him either,' Hannah argued.

'The dog belongs to Danny Jones,' he said quietly but firmly. 'Sorry, girls, but what can we do?'

'Plenty!' Helen said under her breath.

'Lots of things!' Hannah agreed. 'I don't know exactly what, but there's lots of things we can do!'

The kettle had boiled, the tea was brewed, when their mum came home from work.

'I just passed a mad driver in the village!' she told them, flinging her keys on the table. 'He nearly drove smack into me!'

'In a green van?' Hannah asked.

'Yes. How did you know?'

They told her about Danny Jones and Speckle's narrow escape.

'Well, you two should get an early night before we do anything else,' she decided.

'Mum!' Helen longed to be out there combing the hillside for Speckle. She pictured him hiding, waiting until he thought the coast was clear.

'Hannah and I want to go out looking for him!'

'No, I mean it. Give Speckle a chance to find his own way back. If he doesn't, we'll think again in the morning.' Mary Moore had the last word.

So, all evening, while their dad was out at the cricket match, they stared out of the kitchen window, hoping, yet not hoping to see the puppy come trotting down the lane. They went upstairs at eight o'clock and stared again from the top window along the empty, darkening lane. When night fell, they went to bed. But they didn't sleep. They gazed up at the ceiling, watching shadows from the chestnut tree flicker in the moonlight.

'Hannah?' Helen whispered.

'Yes?'

'You haven't changed your mind, have you?'

'What about?' Hannah couldn't think of anything except Speckle.

'You do you want us to find Speckle?' Helen did and she didn't; not if they had to hand him over to cruel Danny Jones. But she shivered at the thought of the dangers on the mountain.

There was a long silence.

'Hannah, do you?'

'Yes,' Hannah decided. Something had come to her in a sudden flash. 'Listen, I've just had an idea. How long is it before it gets light?'

Helen looked at the luminous hands on her watch. 'Hours and hours. Why?'

'Well, in the morning, early, you've got to go out and look for him, right?'

'What about you?'

'We've got to split up. I want to go into Nesfield with Mum.'

To Helen this was unheard of. She and Hannah did everything together, ever since they were tiny. She hated the idea of splitting up. 'Wouldn't it be better for us both to stay and look?' But she knew Hannah inside-out; her sister had a plan. She could tell by the excitement in her voice. 'Come on, Hann, what are you up to?'

'It's not me, it's that Danny Jones. He's the one who's up to something.'

'Maybe it's just that we didn't like him, like Dad said.' Now Helen wasn't so sure. She was suddenly afraid that every word Jones had said was true.

'No, it's more than that. I didn't *trust* him!' She waited for this to sink in. 'So will you go and look for

Speckle while I go into town? And don't let that Danny Jones anywhere near him, OK!'

At last Helen agreed. 'I just hope you're right,' she sighed. 'And I hope Speckle's OK!'

Nine

They tossed and turned all night. The clock in the hallway ticked steadily, shadows flitted across the moon. At dawn they woke. It was Saturday; exactly a week since Ben had found them by the lake and they'd gone up the fell to rescue Speckle from the quarry.

By seven o'clock, Helen was up and dressed. As Hannah got ready to drive into Nesfield with their mum, she made her own plans.

'I want to ask Mr Fox if I can borrow Ben,' she told them over breakfast. 'Do you think he'll let me?'

'What do you want to borrow him for?' David Moore asked.

'To help me find Speckle.'

Hannah stood at the door waiting for her mum to get ready. 'Good luck!' she whispered to Helen.

'You too.' Helen went and picked up Speckle's old checked blanket. Quickly she tore a corner from it and put it in her pocket. She nodded at Hannah and set out across the yard.

She ran downhill to Lakeside Farm. Luckily, John Fox was in. Ben barked at the gate as he heard her footsteps, then he ran quickly to heel as the old farmer came out to see who it was.

Helen was out of breath. She'd run all the way. 'Mr Fox, can I take Ben to help me look for Speckle? He ran off yesterday teatime!'

'Again?' He sniffed and glanced up the fell.

'Yes, but this time it's different. A man came to take him away!' She told him about Danny Jones's visit.

'Jones? I don't know the name,' he said slowly.

'He lives in town. He says Speckle's real name is Prince, and he's coming back to track him down!' She wanted to find him before Jones did. 'If I take Ben with me, I've got more chance!' she begged.

'And what's wrong with this Jones chap?'

'I don't know exactly. Something. Speckle didn't like him. He refused to go!'

John Fox nodded. 'A dog is a pretty good judge of human nature,' he agreed. 'Anyhow, I don't like the idea of a stranger coming up the fell and dragging him off to town if that's not what he wants.'

Helen could see that the farmer was working his way around to saying yes. She waited patiently, ready to spring into action.

'Well, as it happens, I don't need Ben this morning.' He tilted his cap back from his forehead. There was a pause. 'Aye, all right, then.'

'Thanks!' A smile lit up Helen's anxious face. She pulled the scrap of blanket from her shorts pocket and bent forward. 'Here, Ben, sniff this!'

Ben obeyed. His sensitive nose got to work. Helen went to the farm gate. 'Here, boy!'

Ben cocked an ear at her. He looked up at his owner. Mr Fox gave a small nod. Ben raced to the gate.

'OK, good boy.' She showed him the red square again. 'Now, fetch!'

He seemed to understand. Head down, he sniffed this way and that. Then he raised his head to scent the

air. Soon he was off, across fields, heading for open country.

Helen tried to keep up, past Austby Fold and High Hartwell, beyond the high sheep farms on to the grey, stony slopes of the upper fell. Ben went sure-footed and tireless, while she struggled along. Often he would sit and wait, head up, sniffing at the breeze. They listened for any sound, any sign of the lost puppy.

Eventually they came close to the quarry, the scene of the first rescue. Helen recognised the tall rocks and the sheer drop beyond. For a moment she hesitated. Had Ben got it wrong? Surely Speckle had learned his lesson first time round? She peered into the depths of the old stone-working, over the dangerous edge.

But Ben was still at work. He put his nose to the ground, reading the scents, picking up tracks. He gave a sharp bark. Helen looked round. He was trying to lead her off, away from the quarry, still further up the fell.

Helen breathed again. Speckle hadn't blundered into the same trap as before. Ben had a definite trail. He loped ahead, sniffing, then turning to wait.

But her relief turned to alarm when she followed her guide across a rough pathway. There, further down the hill, was the sturdy figure of Danny Jones. He'd carried out his promise to come looking for Speckle. For a second she stood rooted to the spot.

Jones was muttering to himself, wondering which way to take. 'The dratted dog must be here somewhere!' He looked all round. He stood with his hands on his hips, scanning the hillside.

Helen gasped. Soon he would be charging towards her. He mustn't know she was here trying to find poor Speckle before he did. 'Come on, boy!' She called Ben and they darted off the track behind a boulder.

They dipped down a bank, out of sight, splashing through a shallow stream and under the cover of a clump of hawthorn bushes. She heard footsteps crunch nearer.

Jones came to a stop about fifty metres from where they were hidden.

'Which way now?' he muttered to himself.

Helen held her breath. Hiding behind the spiky bushes, with one arm tight around Ben's neck, she stayed hidden. Jones moved nearer, muttering and complaining. His legs and heavy boots passed just feet from where she hid.

'Shh, Ben!' she whispered.

The obedient dog stayed still. The man tramped by. She closed her eyes. At last he was gone.

'Quick! We've got to find Speckle before he does!' She came out with Ben from behind the bushes. Now there was no time to lose.

Ben began working here and there to pick up the scent he'd lost when Jones interrupted him.

At last he found it. Speckle's trail led in the opposite direction to Jones, thank heavens. Ben pressed on, nose to the ground, up and up towards the very top of the mountain.

When they reached it, Helen had to stop for breath. She could see for miles, all along a rocky ridge in one direction, back down into the valley with the lake and Doveton village strung out along its shore. To the right was another valley, another lake with tiny sailing boats curving across its blue surface.

'Where now, Ben?' She could see no sign of the lost dog, way up here on what seemed like the top of the world.

Ben was still busy. He trotted along the ridge, following a narrow footpath worn into the sparse grass.

Helen's heart sank. Ben was taking her along a wild new track. It could take them far from her own valley and Home Farm. How far could Speckle possibly have gone? She was scared, she had to admit, as she set foot on the narrow path.

But Ben was sure. His ears pricked up, he seemed excited. Once or twice he lifted his head to bark. Birds flew up from the shelter of some rocks; a pair of pheasants and a brown one with a curved beak. It curled overhead, calling out a warning. Ben swerved off the path towards the rocks. Helen stopped and watched.

He barked, then he sat in the heather. He barked again, turning to look at her.

'Ben?' She took a step or two off the track into the thick bank of heather. It scratched her legs, tugged at her feet. She stopped to listen. 'Speckle?' she called softly.

There was a rustling in the heather, a flash of white.

'Speckle!' This time her voice was louder.

A shape bounded out of the sea of purple heather; black and white, with the telltale speckled legs. He yelped and barked, overjoyed to see them both after his long night all alone. He tumbled as the heather caught his legs. He rolled and jumped to his feet. Helen and Ben ran towards him. They'd found him! Now they had to get him safely back to Home Farm without bumping into Danny Jones. They would wait there until Hannah came back from town.

'Speckle!' She tried to scold him. She caught him in her arms. Ben leapt round, herding them back on to the ridge. She half-laughed, half-cried to have him safe.

Quickly they set off down the fell towards Doveton, Ben leading the way. She kept a close lookout for Danny. Their luck was in; he'd obviously taken a different path and they made it home without being seen.

She ran into the house ahead of the two dogs, calling for her dad. 'We found him! Here he is! Is Hannah back yet?' she cried in one breath. Now everything depended on Hannah; Speckle's whole life and chance of happiness.

Ten

The windows of The Curlew Cafe in Nesfield shone bright in the morning sun. Hannah followed her mum inside.

'How long have we got?' she asked.

Mary Moore handed her a thick telephone directory. 'About half an hour. Sophie comes in at nine, and I have to be here to help her.' Saturday was a busy day in the cafe, but she'd promised to help Hannah carry out her plan. 'Can you find the address?'

Hannah ran down the list. 'Jones, A., Jones, C. J., Jones, D. Here he is! Number 14c High Street,

Nesfield!' She'd heard him say that he lived on the High Street; now they had the number of the house.

Her mum checked. '14c? It sounds like a flat.'

'Come on, let's go!' She was eager to be off, dying to check up on a few of Danny Jones's facts.

They left the cafe and walked quickly into the town centre.

Nesfield was waking up to a busy market day. Stalls were up in the main square, vans delivered fruit and vegetables, shoppers began to trickle in. The High Street ran from one corner of the square. Hannah and her mum hurried towards it, past pretty shop fronts selling postcards and walking gear.

'This is it!' Hannah read the street sign.

But someone was calling Mary Moore from across the street. 'It's Sophie,' she said. 'Look, I'll just have to stop for a minute to explain what's happening, OK?'

Hannah nodded. 'I'll go on ahead.'

'Well, take care.' Her mum crossed the street to talk to the wavy-haired teenager who helped out at the cafe.

Hannah went on. They were big houses set well

back from the road. The first four houses were made into hotels, with wide drives and bright signs. The traffic flowed down the street towards the square.

At last she came to number 14. It was a small block of flats, two storeys high, with a flat roof, and space for parked cars. Hannah looked carefully. *Good! Danny Jones's van isn't here!* She was glad he wasn't around to interfere.

Now she had to wait for someone to come out of the flats. Seconds ticked by. At last, a middle-aged lady in a blue shirt and black trousers came out of a side door, shopping-basket in hand.

Hannah took a deep breath. She'd rehearsed this over and over; she knew exactly what she wanted to ask.

She stepped forward to introduce herself. The woman looked friendly, with a warm smile and time to listen. She looked closely at Hannah. 'Moore? You belong to the new people at The Curlew, don't you?'

Hannah nodded, then began. 'I'd like to know if one of your neighbours has a dog,' she said nervously.

The woman frowned as she thought for a while. 'You must mean Danny Jones?'

Hannah nodded. He was telling the truth, then; he *did* own a dog. She'd been sure the answer would be no, that Jones would turn out to be lying. Disappointed, she pressed on nevertheless. 'What colour? What sort is he?'

'Black and white, as far as I remember. Some type of collie. Prince; that's the name. Why? What's all this about?' The woman's curiosity raced on. She set her basket on the wall and turned back to Hannah.

'Does he have speckles?' This was their last chance; if the woman said yes, she really would have to give in. It meant Danny Jones was telling the truth.

'Speckles?' There was a long pause. 'No, I don't think so.'

Hannah's eyes widened. She held her breath. 'No speckles on his legs, here?' She brushed up and down her own arms.

'No, and anyway . . .' The woman seemed confused. 'Why do you want to know?'

Hannah spilled out the story. 'Danny Jones came up to our farm last night. He says he's lost a dog. And we've found a dog in the quarry, and he says it's his. But I don't think it is, so we came here to try and find out!'

The woman put up her hands. 'Slow down, let's get this straight. Danny claims your dog is his?' She shook her head.

'Could it be?' she asked.

'No, that can't be right,' the woman answered.

'Why not?' Hannah rushed on with her questions.

'Well, you see, Danny's dog, Prince, can't be the same dog. The poor little thing was run over on the main road here, just last week. He ran out into the traffic and was killed. It was very sad.'

Tears sprang to Hannah's eyes. 'So Danny Jones doesn't have a dog?'

'Not any more. We knew it wasn't really right to keep a dog here. He's only got a tiny flat, and there was nowhere for it to run about. Dogs like that need lots of exercise.' She could have talked on, but something drew her up short. 'Are you all right?' she asked Hannah. 'I thought you'd be pleased.'

'I am,' she said through her tears.

She thanked the woman. Now she was quite clear; Danny Jones's collie puppy had been killed in an accident, poor thing. He was playing a trick on them by coming to Home Farm and claiming that Speckle was his.

'I expect he thought he'd get something for nothing,' the neighbour told her. 'He's that sort, I'm afraid.'

Again she thanked her.

'Think nothing of it. I wouldn't want to see him in charge of another dog, not in that tiny flat of his.'

Smiling, Hannah left the woman and hurried back to find her mum. She bumped into her at the top of the High Street and told her the good news.

'What a relief!' Mary Moore took a deep breath. 'I was just telling Sophie what you and Helen had in mind. She's gone ahead to open up the cafe. Come on, let's go and find her!'

Together they cut across the square towards The Curlew.

Hannah's mum went inside to ask Sophie to look after the place for her. 'I have to take Hannah home. You don't mind?'

Sophie stepped in with a smile. 'Well done,' she grinned at Hannah. 'Your hunch really paid off. And no, of course I don't mind holding the fort.'

'I'll be back as soon as I can.' Mary Moore hurried Hannah into the car. 'We've got to see a man about a dog!'

Sophie rolled up her sleeves and turned the sign on the door to 'Open'. She pointed at the 'Found' notice in the window. 'I take it this can come down now?'

'Yes!' Hannah yelled back. She felt on top of the world. 'Yes, please!'

They arrived at Home Farm just as Danny Jones's green van drove ahead of them into the yard.

Jones got out of the van and slammed the door. He strode to the front door and knocked loudly.

Inside the house, Helen's heart dropped through her boots. Speckle lay on his blanket whining; Ben growled as her dad went to answer the door.

'Danny Jones,' she said to herself. The knock was loud and rude; *rat-tat-rat-tat*. He'd come to claim 'his' dog.

'I've been up on that fell since the crack of dawn,' Jones was saying. 'The dog's not there. I've come to see if he made his way back here.'

David Moore answered quietly. 'No, he didn't.'

Good for you, Dad! Helen's heart missed a beat.

But he was bracing himself to tell the truth. 'As a matter of fact, one of the twins went to fetch him.'

She let out a groan. Why did she have to have an honest dad?

'You mean, she found him?' Jones was taken aback. Then he pulled himself together. 'Come on, then, hand him over!'

Helen crept up behind her father. She saw the big man, and behind him, Hannah and her mum. They were running.

'Stop!' Hannah, the gentle, sensible one, came shoving against the six-foot man. Speckle heard her voice and ran to the door. Danny Jones bent to swipe him into his arms. 'Have you got Speckle? Don't let him go!' Hannah yelled. She was breathless and fierce.

Helen scooped the puppy from the floor before Jones could grab him. She backed into the safety of the kitchen, with Ben growling a warning at the stranger not to come any further.

'Speckle isn't yours!' Hannah stood face to face with Jones. 'You haven't got a dog. Yours was killed in an accident! We heard all about it!'

Helen felt a surge of victory. 'I knew it!' She gestured to Hannah to come through the door. Together they stood guard with Ben in front of the puppy.

Danny Jones backed off. 'All right, all right.' He

shoved his hands into his pockets. 'You win.' He admitted the whole thing. 'What harm was I doing?' He shrugged it off. 'You'd found a dog. I wanted another one. It's no big deal, is it?'

'You lied!' Helen wasn't ready to forgive him. She remembered how rough he'd been, trying to grab Speckle in the yard the day before.

Jones turned red. 'Well.' He shuffled from one foot to the other. 'You could still give me the dog. Like I said, it makes sense.'

It was Mary Moore's turn to speak. 'No, I don't think so.' She sounded absolutely sure. 'That's out of the question.' She looked him straight in the eye. 'I don't trust you to take care of any dog properly.'

At that moment the twins would have entered her for Mum of the Year. She would have won. She was their heroine.

Danny Jones couldn't meet her gaze. 'Look,' he said, still shuffling, 'it was a trick, I admit it.'

They stood waiting. No one helped him off the hook.

'OK, then, I'm sorry,' he muttered. 'OK? Sorry. Sorry!' He backed off mumbling, 'I didn't mean any harm, OK?'

They stared. Speckle came to the door, thrust his head between a sea of legs and barked. It broke the silence.

David Moore relented first. 'All right, we accept your apology,' he told Danny Jones. 'All's well that ends well, after all!' He even went so far as to shake hands.

It left Danny Jones speechless. Covered in confusion, he beat it back to the van. 'Well done girls,' David Moore smiled. 'His cheap trick has backfired. I don't think Danny Jones will bother us again.'

Speckle seemed to know that he owed it all to Ben and the twins. For days he followed Helen and Hannah everywhere they went; upstairs into the attic to help their dad mend the roof, out in the farmyard digging up weeds and planting more flowers with their mum. He got under their feet and into tight corners. Helen even rescued him from the inside of the washing-machine! Hannah found him diving into the dustbin and had to haul him out.

People in the village got used to seeing them out together, the frisky puppy and the dark-haired, live-wire twins. Everyone got to hear the story of Danny Jones and his mean trick.

'Here, give the pup a biscuit.' Luke Martin offered a tidbit from a box under the counter. 'And take an ice-cream each from the freezer. I reckon you deserve it!'

They bathed in their success, lapped up the praise. The village treated them like heroes. Even Mr Winter stopped them to ask after Speckle.

'Now, I hope you're going to train that dog properly!' he said sternly. He stood to attention at his garden gate. Speckle was on his best behaviour and Puppy was the one spoiling for a fight. The schoolteacher's terrier growled a warning from his front doorstep.

The twins told him that Speckle was already in training.

'Sit!' Helen gave him a signal and the command. He sat like an angel.

Like a champion sheepdog! Hannah thought proudly. She walked on a few steps. 'Here!' she called. He flew at her command.

Puppy leapt down the steps and cleared the garden wall with one bound. He was a bundle of yapping fur and sharp teeth. 'Puppy!' Mr Winter's sharp cry went unheeded.

'Here, Speckle!' Helen showed him how it was done. Their puppy side-stepped the terrier and followed them meekly down the street.

They went along, heads high, while Mr Winter struggled with his snappy pet.

'. . . Aye,' John Fox said, when they laughed over the incident with him. 'He has no idea how to control that dog, that's the trouble.' He was leaning on their gate, the one their dad still hadn't got round to mending. It was the end of the spring holiday. Tomorrow was another fresh start; their first day at a new school.

The farmer let Ben into the yard to play with Speckle. 'You've not had any more phone calls about the puppy then?'

Hannah shook her head. 'Mum says now that Speckle was definitely abandoned. She doesn't think anyone wants him, not after all this time.'

'Hmm.' Mr Fox cast an expert eye over Speckle. 'He's shaping up nicely, now he's put on weight.' There was a shrewd note in his voice, as David Moore came out to say hello. 'I was just saying, I could make a decent working dog out of that pup, given half a chance!' He tipped back his cap and scratched his head. 'I reckon he'll make a good farm dog once he's fully grown.'

'He's changed his tune,' Helen whispered to Hannah. Wasn't it Mr Fox who called Speckle a useless townie? Still, she felt proud.

'I don't suppose you'd let me have a go at making something of him?' the old farmer dropped in.

David Moore laughed. 'You'd better ask them!' He pointed to Helen and Hannah.

'No thanks!' They gave their answer smart and prompt. If Speckle was going to be a champion, they were the ones who were going to put in the hard work and take the glory.

'Aye well, worth a try!'

'Speckle's a champion to us in any case!' Hannah spoke up for them all. 'And he likes it here at Home Farm, doesn't he, Dad?'

'He sure does.' Her dad folded his arms and gazed all around.

Home Farm, the fell, the nearby village. The twins smiled at their mum as she came out into the warm afternoon sun.

'So, you've settled in?' John Fox nodded his approval.

They all agreed that they had.

'That's grand, then. It's good to see the old place full of life again.' The farmer glanced towards his Land-Rover parked in the lane. 'I brought something for you.' He stumped off and came back with a wooden crate. Speckle and Ben came running to investigate. 'I thought the girls might want to rear a few chicks,' he said gruffly. He didn't want them to think he'd gone soft.

Helen and Hannah gasped with delight. Mr Fox lifted the lid of the crate. Inside were six fluffy yellow chicks, cheeping and blinking at the sudden bright light.

'Would you?' their mum asked with a smile.

'Yes!' they cried. Chickens in the farmyard, a dog in the kitchen. 'Yes! Yes!'

'OK,' their dad agreed. 'Why not? I suppose all the jobs can wait while we get young Speckle trained and these chickens nicely settled down!' He winked at the twins.

Speckle jumped at the crate to peer inside. He toppled in amongst the chicks. Hannah rescued him just in time. The chicks peeped and cheeped.

'Oh, and by the way,' John Fox rumbled on, as Helen scooped one tiny chick into the palm of her hand, 'I hear that Fred Hunt at High Hartwell is looking for a good home for a litter of kittens . . .'

The twins shot longing glances at their mum.

'No!' Mary Moore stepped in firmly. 'Thank you, John!'

He gave one of his barking laughs. 'Aye, well,' he shrugged, then he winked at the twins. 'No harm in asking!'

He went off with Ben, down to Lakeside Farm. Their dad was busy looking up chicken coops and kennels in his do-it-yourself book. Meanwhile, their mum had taken charge of the chicks. She'd put them on a ledge in the kitchen, 'Out of harm's way,' she said, meaning Speckle.

So the twins sat outside with their dog. *Their champion*. They would take down all the Found notices, and Speckle would be theirs at last.

He snuggled up, stretching over both their laps, in the shade of the chestnut tree.

'Wherever we go, you go too,' they told him. Lazily he wagged his tail. 'You live here at Home Farm. This is where you belong!'